Mike the Genius

CARAMEL TREE

Chapter 1

Study and Study

Mike is a student.
He is a smart student.
Mike is a genius!

Mike always studies.
He studies and studies.

Mike has a big test soon.
He studies science.
He studies and studies.

$$f(x) = ax^2 + bx + c = 0$$

$$x_1 = \frac{-b + \sqrt{b^2 - 4ac}}{2a}$$

$$\frac{-b - \sqrt{b^2 - 4ac}}{2a}$$

$\sin A$

$\sum_{i=1}^{n} w_i n (x_i)$

$ax + bx$

Mike has a big test soon.
He studies math.
He studies and studies.

Mike has a big test soon.
He studies maps.
Big maps. Small maps.
Maps. Maps. Maps.

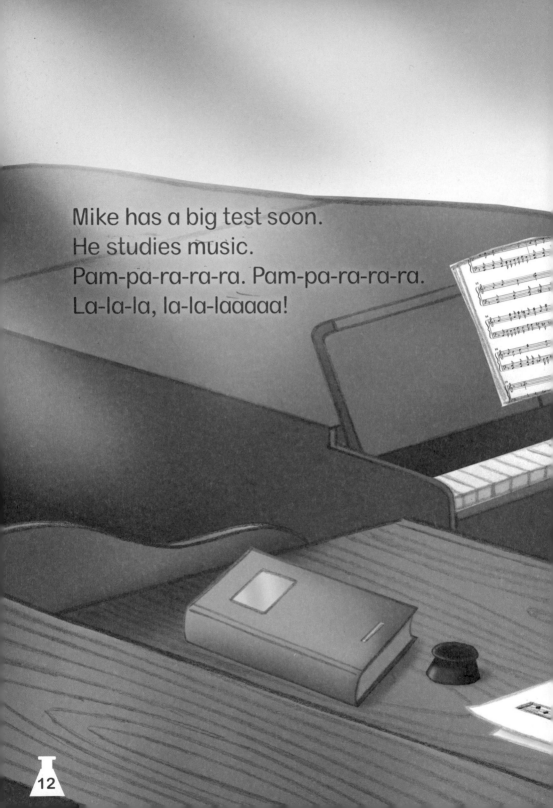

Mike has a big test soon.
He studies music.
Pam-pa-ra-ra-ra. Pam-pa-ra-ra-ra.
La-la-la, la-la-laaaaa!

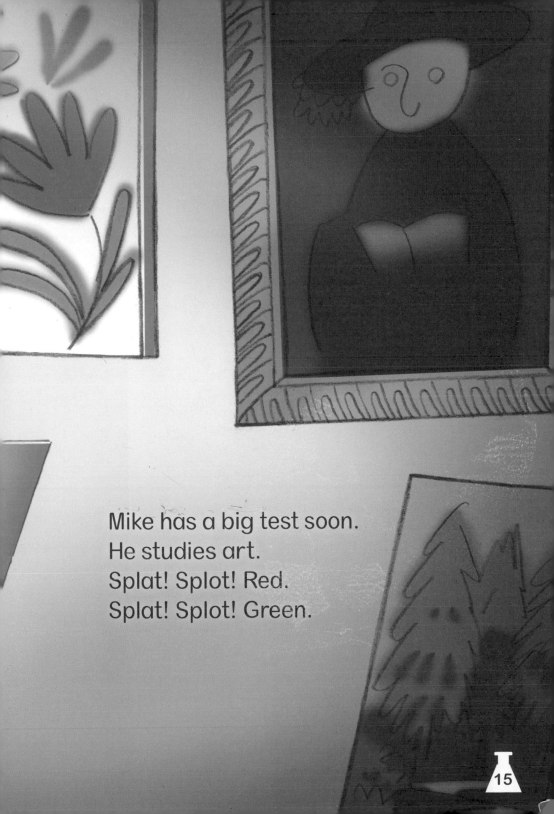

Mike has a big test soon.
He studies art.
Splat! Splot! Red.
Splat! Splot! Green.

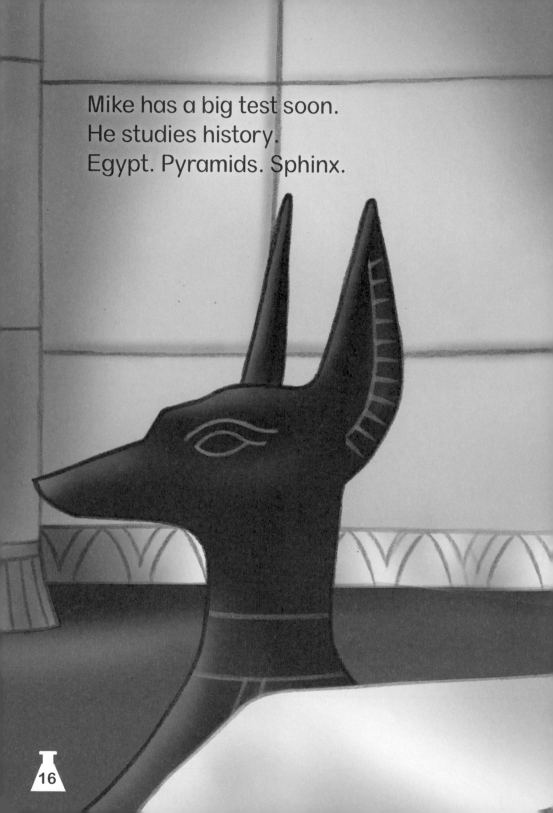

Mike has a big test soon.
He studies history.
Egypt. Pyramids. Sphinx.

Chapter 3

Read and Write

Mike sits in the library.
He reads many books.
He reads and reads.

19

Mike has many notebooks.
He writes in all his notebooks.
He writes and writes.

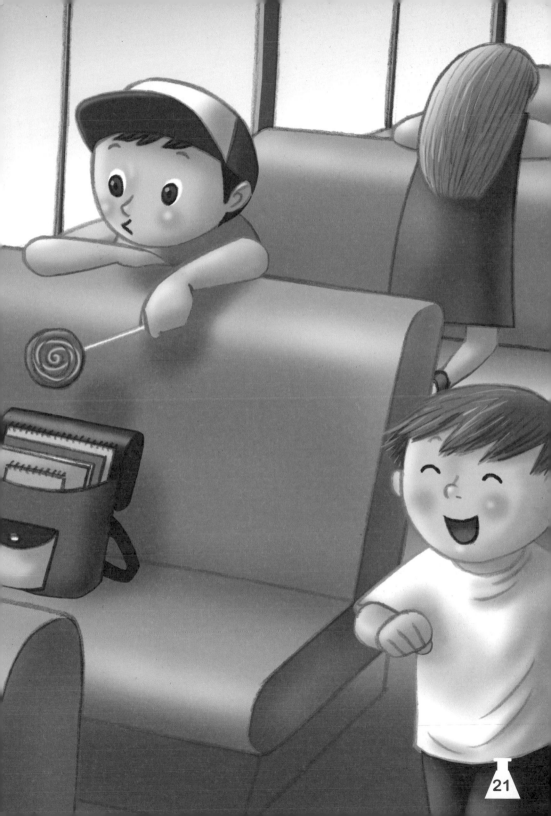

Mike does his homework.
He studies and studies.
Tick-tock! Tick-tock!

Mike studies science and math.
3-2-1! Correct! Hooray!

Mike studies maps and music.
Pam-pa-ra-ra-ra. La-la-laaaaa!

Mike studies art and history.
Splat! Splot! Red. Green.

29

It is the test day.
"Where is Mike today?" says the teacher.

"We do not know," say the students.

"Let's start the test," says the teacher.

Oh no! Mike is sleeping in his bed.

Mike is missing the test!